INSIDE MOUSE, OUTSIDE MOUSE

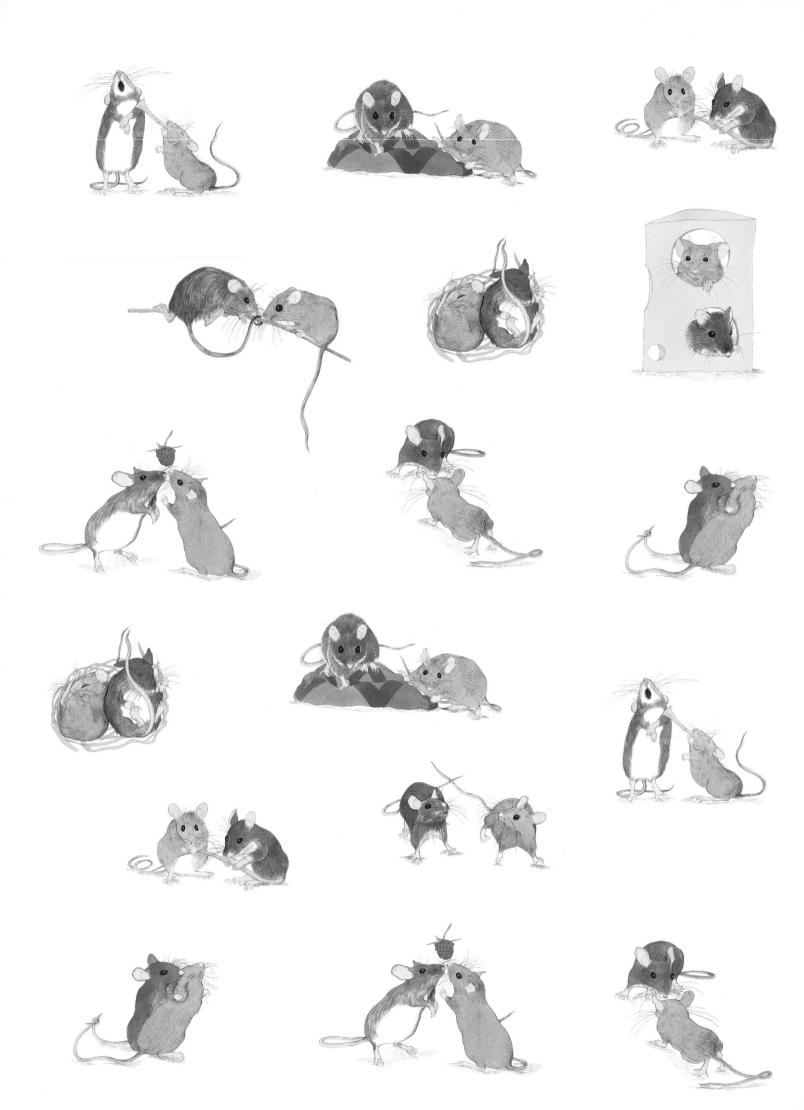

Lindsay Barrett George

INSIDE MOUSE, OUTSIDE MOUSE

SCHOLASTIC INC.
New York Toronto London Auckland Sydney
Mexico City New Delhi Hong Kong Buenos Aires

Inside my house
there is a mouse,

Outside my house
there is a mouse,

who sleeps in a clock.

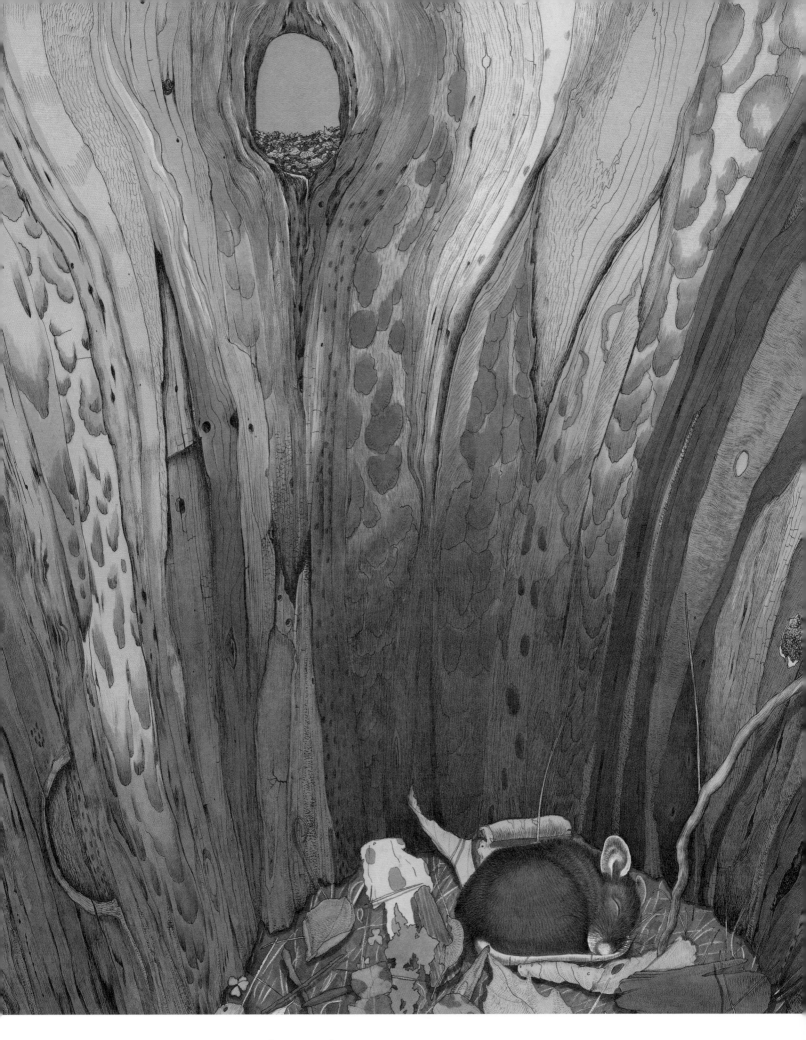

who sleeps in a stump.

The mouse ran down the wall,

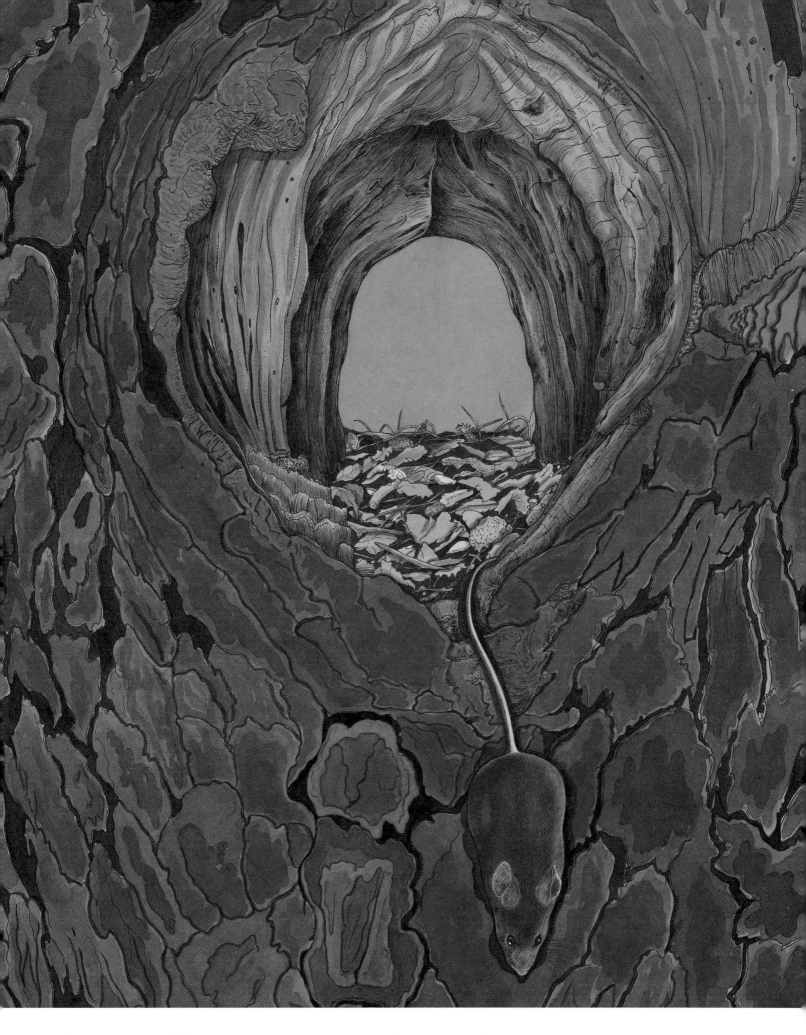

The mouse ran down the stump,

across the rug,

across the ground,

under the table, next to the cat.

under the bush, next to the hare.

He ran up the chair,

He ran up the wall,

in front of the dog,

in front of the squirrel,

into the can and out of the can.

into the can and out of the can.

He ran behind the book,

He ran behind the bird,

between the socks,

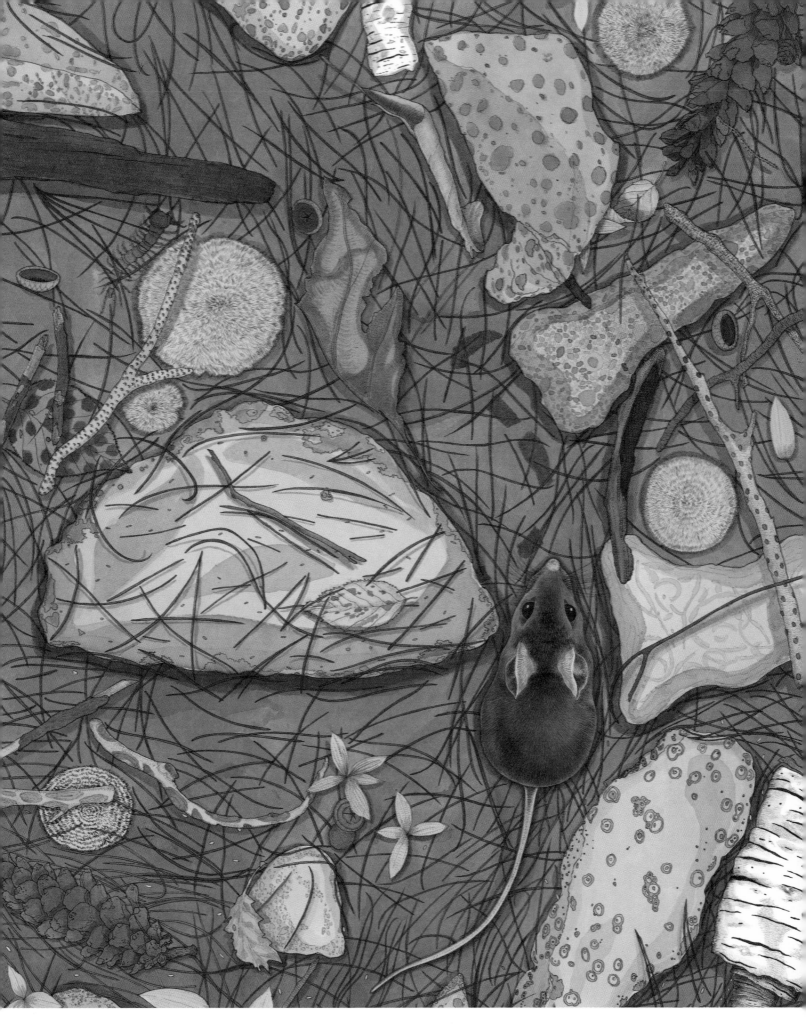

between the rocks,

below the spider, and over the ball.

below the spider, and over the stone.

He ran through the hole,

He ran through the hole,

along the bat,

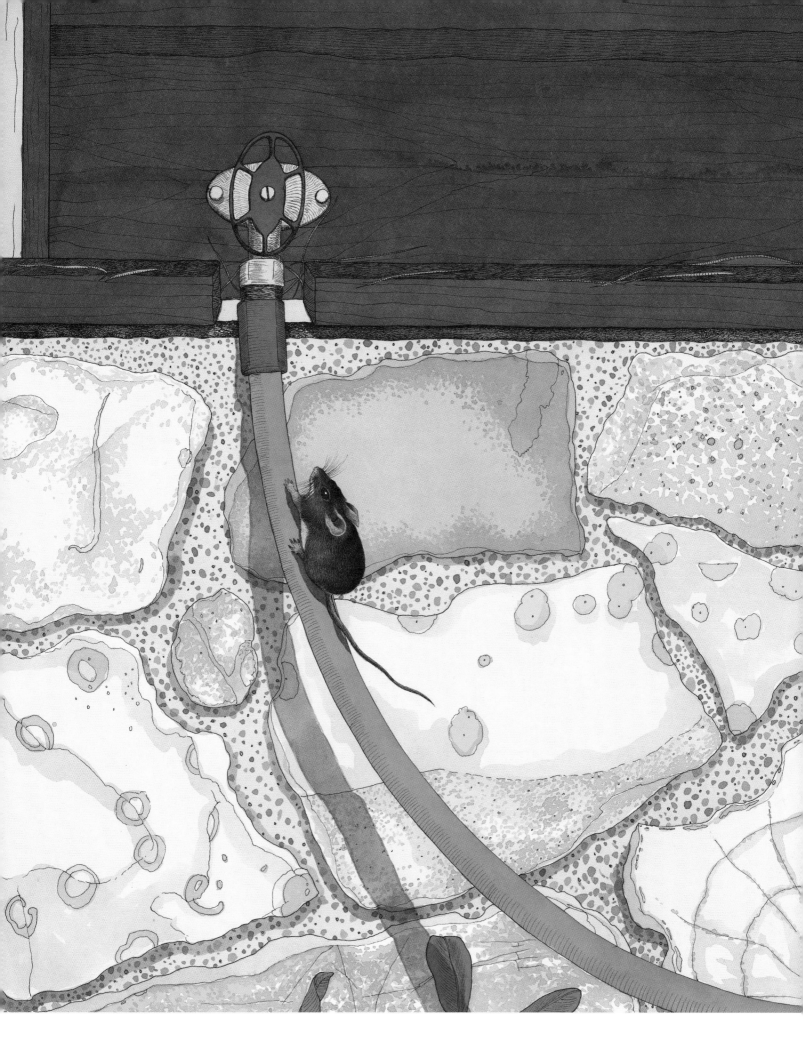

along the hose,

around the flowers, and stopped . . .

around the flowers, and stopped . . .

to look outside my house.

to look inside my house.

For Virginia
Thank you for giving me my voice.

—L. B. G.

ISBN 0-439-85800-3

Copyright © 2004 by Lindsay Barrett George. All rights reserved.
Published by Scholastic Inc., 557 Broadway, New York, NY 10012,
by arrangement with Greenwillow Books, an imprint of HarperCollins Publishers.
SCHOLASTIC and associated logos are trademarks and/or registered trademarks of Scholastic Inc.

12 11 10 9 8 7 6 5 4 3 2 1   6 7 8 9 10 11/0

Printed in the U.S.A.   08

First Scholastic printing, April 2006
Gouache paints were used to prepare the full-color art.
The text of this book is set in GoudySans.